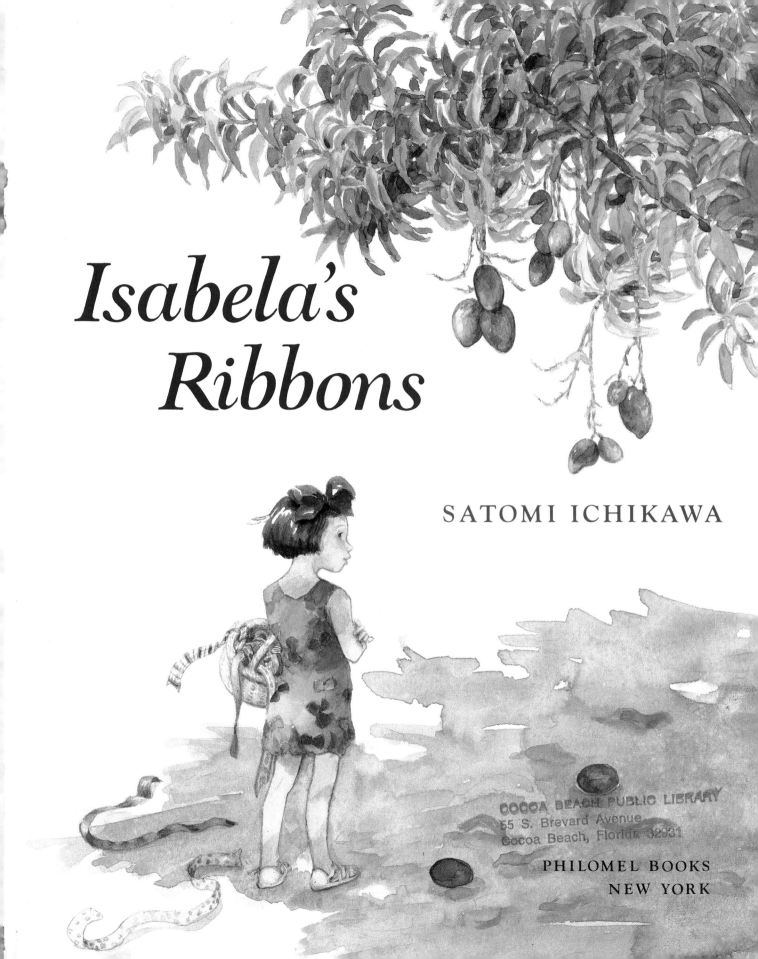

Isabela's
Ribbons

SATOMI ICHIKAWA

PHILOMEL BOOKS
NEW YORK

For my Puerto Rican aunt,
"Titita" Liliana San Juan Gonzalez Giusti,
and her granddaughter Isabel-Elena

Philomel Books, Reg. U.S. Pat. & Tm. Off. Published simultaneously in Canada. Printed in Singapore.
Book design by Gunta Alexander. The text is set in Goudy Old Style.
Library of Congress Cataloging-in-Publication Data
Ichikawa, Satomi.   Isabela's ribbons / Satomi Ichikawa.   p.   cm.
Summary: A little Puerto Rican girl uses her basket full of colorful ribbons to help her hide and to help
her make some new friends.   [1. Ribbons—Fiction. 2. Hide-and-seek—Fiction. 3. Puerto Rico—Fiction.]
I. Title.   PZ7.I16Is   1995   [E]—dc20   94-43032   CIP   AC   ISBN 0-399-22772-5

1   3   5   7   9   10   8   6   4   2
First Impression

There is an island in the ocean where the sun shines all year long. Flowers bloom in bright colors, sweet fruits hang from the trees, and all the little girls wear ribbons in their hair. Here is one of their stories.

*O*nce, there was a little girl who lived on an island. Her name was Isabela. She loved ribbons of every color and wore them wherever she went. Isabela had never been seen without a ribbon. "Hello, Ribbon Lady," people would wave their hands and say.

Every day Isabela tied a ribbon in her hair and went to play outside.

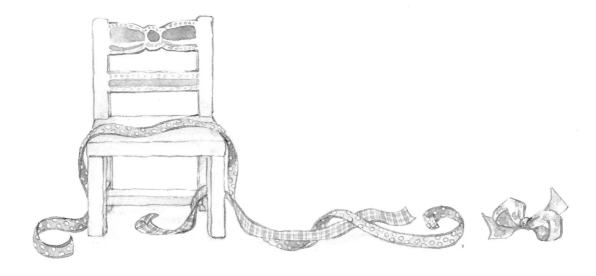

Isabela's favorite game was hide-and-seek. How she loved to play with her dog, Samantha.

She hid among the pink hibiscus flowers so well that
Samantha couldn't find her!

Sometimes she played with her neighbor Patria in the
banana tree.

"Hello, Ribbon Lady! Where are you?" Patria would call,
but she could not find Isabela.

Sometimes Isabela
played with her grandma.
"I will find you, my little
Isabela," Grandma would sing.
Grandma would search
and search the blooming red
flamboyant tree, but she could
not find Isabela.

Isabela loved playing hide-and-seek.
But one day nobody wanted to play with
Isabela. Grandma had friends visiting, Patria
went shopping with friends, even Samantha
had a friend to play with.

Isabela had no friends to play
with her, so she took a basket full of
ribbons and went to play alone.

Inside the mango tree, the thick leaves made a fine hiding place, but how could she play hide-and-seek alone? Playing her favorite game wasn't any fun today.

Suddenly someone squawked at her. It was a parrot, come to eat a mango. Delighted, Isabela said, "Hello, parrot. Would you play hide-and-seek with me? I'll hide first." And Isabela waved the parrot away.

Quickly, she tied her ribbons all over the tree
and hid among them. Never would the parrot find
her. Isabela held her breath and waited. And waited.
But the parrot did not come back.

Inside the tree, it seemed cooler and quieter,
like being underneath the sea.

All at once Isabela found herself in that deep sea, and
the ribbons were fish of every color! Isabela was a fish too.

Together they swam into the middle of the sea.
They swam along reefs of coral and past hidden islands.
They swam and swam. Then Isabela saw a bright light.
"Let's swim to the sunlight," she said, and she and the
fish swam together.

Isabela looked through the sunlight and saw many children playing. How she wished she and her fish could swim to them. She wanted to share her fish.

"Swim, fish," she said to them. "Swim!"

When the children looked up, they stopped playing.
What they saw were ribbons of every color flying out of
the mango tree! Delighted, they chased the ribbons and
grabbed at them and caught them.

Finally, they discovered Isabela hiding behind the
mango tree.

Now Isabela has many friends to play with, and they all love ribbons as much as Isabela. But now there are so many ribbons that some days Patria still cannot find her Ribbon Lady!

As for Isabela, she loves
her ribbons more than ever.